To Elyse + Tyler
Merry Christmas!
2006

Enjoy!
Frank Barrish

D1200156

Pancho and the Power

This is the desert near where Grandpa lives in New Mexico.

Pancho and the Power

Story and Photography
by Frank H. Parrish

Published by
Barbed Wire Publishing
270 Avenida de Mesilla
Las Cruces, New Mexico 88005 USA
www.barbed-wire.net

Paperback ISBN 0-9678566-2-0
Hard cover ISBN 0-9678566-4-7

2 3 4 5 6 7 8 9 0

Second Printing: August 2002

To the ultimate Power,
and Karl, a wild coyote
who carried the message.

"*F*rancisco, get up! You'll be late for the bus if you don't hurry."

Suddenly, wide awake, he jumped out of bed.

"You mean he is still in bed?" his father spoke sharply. "Frank, your breakfast is sure to be cold by now, if your sisters haven't eaten it already."

"Francisco, get going this minute!" his mother scolded. She only called him "Francisco" when her patience was wearing thin.

Frank pulled on his worn, but newly pressed pants and his favorite calico shirt in record time. "I'm ready," he said as he scurried into the tiny kitchen past his mother, snatched a still warm tortilla from under its cover, spooned out the last of the scrambled eggs and green chiles and rolled them into the tortilla, making a burrito. Then he headed for the door.

"Wait, you forgot your homework," his mother called. "Now hurry and catch up with your sisters."

It was a long bus ride to school and Frank was glad his mother hadn't let him forget his homework. His report on nature was due today. Frank chose to write about the Horned Toad, a most unusual lizard.

The bus pulled up to the school with just enough time, as always, to get off and meet his friend, Albert. Then the first bell rang and off they went to the classroom, hurrying to beat the tardy bell.

Most of the students lived in Las Cruces, but many, like Frank and his friend Albert, lived on farms or ranches in the Mesilla Valley along the Rio Grande; some came from ranches in the Robledo or the Organ Mountains.

"All right class, be seated," the teacher said. "Pass your homework forward. When I call you, come up and get your paper and read your report." Frank was glad he had finished his homework on time, even though the teacher never called on him to give his report the same day they were due. The teacher had collected and stacked the reports and was sorting through them. "The first report today will be Frank's on the Horned Toad!"

Nearly two months had passed since the day of the class reports. Frank and Albert spent most of their free time roaming in the arroyos and canyons searching for animal tracks, different kinds of rocks, and strange kinds of

cactus. One late afternoon they were walking in the arroyo across the mountain ridge where Frank lived, and in the damp sand they saw some animal tracks. "Look!" said Albert, "They lead to the waterhole!"

Frank studied the tracks carefully and said, "Albert,

there is something very different about these tracks. Look! Here's another set of tracks, only a lot bigger."

Sure enough, only five feet from the first set of tracks was a second set of larger tracks. "I'll bet they're wolves' tracks."

"Nah, can't be," said Albert.

"Look how big this set of tracks is," said Frank. "I never saw a coyote track this big. Maybe it's a

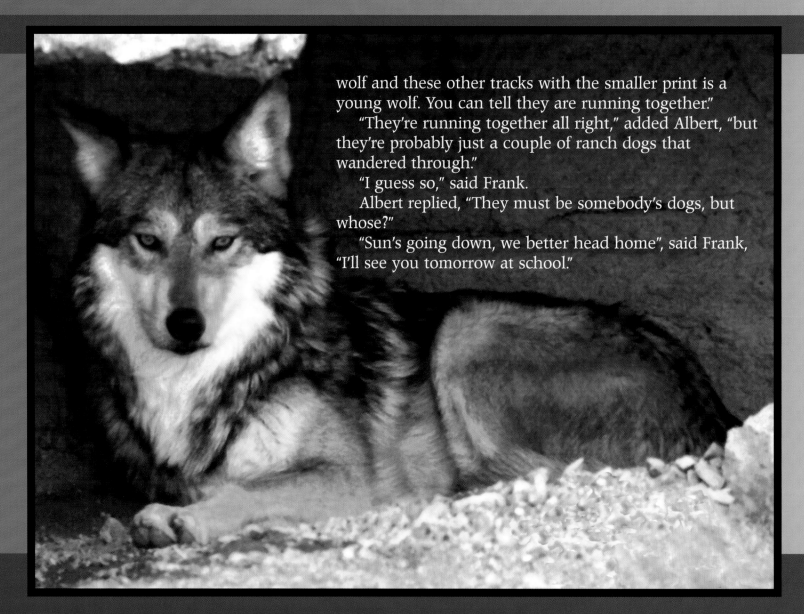

wolf and these other tracks with the smaller print is a young wolf. You can tell they are running together."

"They're running together all right," added Albert, "but they're probably just a couple of ranch dogs that wandered through."

"I guess so," said Frank.

Albert replied, "They must be somebody's dogs, but whose?"

"Sun's going down, we better head home", said Frank, "I'll see you tomorrow at school."

Frank crossed the arroyo, climbed over the ridge and was walking down the road towards home when a dusty, beat up old pickup came bouncing down the hill. It was Old Man Gardner who owned a large ranch near Frank's home. "Hey, Pancho, you seen my boy, Rod?" he yelled as he slammed on the brakes. Mr. Gardner called Frank *Pancho*, his Spanish nickname. "That boy ain't worth a hoot," he said. "He don't want to be a rancher, that's for sure."

Mr. Gardner had four sons—three of them were now grown and not one of them came back to the ranching life once they left. Everyone knew Old Man Gardner was as tough as nails and every bit the independent man the West was famous for a hundred years ago.

"Get in," he said, "I'll drop you off. Save you a half-mile walk anyway." Frank didn't know Mr. Gardner, except by sight and reputation; but he knew he was probably close to seventy years old and hard to understand. He also knew that he had been a rancher all his life and had come from a ranching family. The thought of the strange animal tracks made Frank want to ask Mr. Gardner what he thought.

"How are your cattle doing this year, Mr. Gardner?" Frank asked.

"Somewhat better than last year; more rain, less sickness."

"Had many losses?" Frank asked.

"Always have losses, but not so bad. Cattle need carin' for. Ain't smart like some animals."

"Ever have losses due to mountain lions?" asked Frank, trying not to show his interest.

"Ain't got no lion problem, that's for sure. Won't have, either—not for very long, that is."

"You get rid of them pretty fast—shoot 'em I mean?" Frank asked.

"I get rid of them, all right. But I usually don't need to get my rifle out. Had a few lions the last ten years, but got rid of 'em. A wildlife fella worked with me on that problem.

"That wildlife fella told me he'd help me move 'em, if I was interested. Told me if it didn't work and they came back, I could always pick up the rifle. He said no self-respecting lion wanted to live on a cattle ranch. Lions don't like people much. Prefer eatin'

deer to cattle. Sometimes they need a little help gettin' relocated. Hunger is their basic need that must be met.

"Maybe that's what's wrong with them boys of mine. They ain't never been hungry. I mean, really hungry like me when I was young, or them lions. Maybe I made it too easy for my boys. They ain't bad boys. They're just different from me. Maybe I was too hard on them all those years and just as soon as they could, they left me and the ranch.

"I built a big herd and a good ranch so they could have it when I'm gone. Now they don't want me or the ranch. That's gratitude for you!

"Doc says I ain't got long in this world. Bad heart, bad kidneys. Never believed nothin' no doc ever said. I do now, though. I've seen my health failin' fast over the last year, especially since about Christmas last.

"Gonna change my will this weekend. I think I'll leave the ranch to the Boy Scouts, maybe, or maybe that wildlife outfit that helped me with the lions. Turn it back to the wolves and the rattlesnakes, like it was when I was a boy."

"Wolves! You had wolves?" Frank asked.

"Shor' did. Lobos, they was called—Gray Wolves. Stockman's nightmare, they were. Got rid of 'em. Ain't seen a wolf sign, let alone no wolf, in fifty years or better, but I sure remember 'em!"

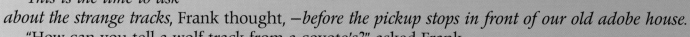

This is the time to ask about the strange tracks, Frank thought, —*before the pickup stops in front of our old adobe house.*

"How can you tell a wolf track from a coyote's?" asked Frank.

"Show me your hand, son." He looked at Frank's open hand and remarked, "you've got small hands for a boy your size. A wolf track would cover half your hand or better. Even a young wolf has huge feet. Easy to track."

Slowing to a stop, he told Frank to ask his papa if he might trade some of his hot red chiles for some fresh beef. "Ask your ma if she still makes that carne seca. If she'll make me some, I'll throw in some extra beef for your family—good beef, too." Then, off clattered the dusty, old pickup toward Las Cruces.

After school the next day, Frank and Albert headed for the water hole, near where they'd seen the tracks. "Hey, we got a three day weekend!" Albert said. "There's some kind of teachers' conference all day Monday. Maybe we could explore this arroyo and follow it up the canyon and see what's up there. Maybe we should ride the horses."

Frank's dad kept two old horses, too old and tired for much except eatin' and sleepin'. "Those tracks we saw gotta be coyotes," Frank said. "Old Man Gardner said wolf tracks are much larger, and he is always watchin' for wolf signs. He says there ain't been a wolf in Doña Ana County in fifty years, but he remembers when there were. He got rid of 'em—or at least did his part—and

Gambel's quail, a roadrunner, and a spotted ground squirrel; but no dogs or coyotes. "I can't sit here any more," said Albert. "It's a waste of time and my dad's been gettin' on me about my chores not gettin' done. Let's go. I'm tired of waitin' for nothin' to happen."

there ain't no wolves in all of New Mexico any more, except an occasional few, down in the Bootheel on the Mexican Border."

"Hey look! Here's those big tracks again. They gotta be dogs," said Albert.

"I'm not so sure," said Frank.

Most of that three-day weekend was spent hiding in the bushes near the waterhole, waiting motionless and silent. Lots of animals came by: rabbits, a badger,

As they headed out of the arroyo and over the ridge for the road that headed toward home, they saw in the far distance a thick dust trail marking the approach of an old truck. As they continued to walk, the truck got closer until finally they could hear the noisy banging of the truck as it bounced over the washboard road.

"It's Old Man Gardner," Frank said.

"Hey! You boys seen my son, Rod?" the old man called.

"No sir," Frank replied.

"That boy just ain't gonna make a rancher, I just gotta accept that. I'm plum wore out. I sent him to Las Cruces to get some tools to work on the windmills. That was around eleven. Darn near four o'clock now. Already fixed the windmill. Don't need them tools now—or that boy. Hop in. I'll drop you by. I gotta get in to see Doc Miller. Been havin' a few spells here lately, ain't feelin' too good."

As the truck neared Frank's place, Mr. Gardner slowed down to a coast and pulled up toward the old adobe house.

"You boys deer hunters?" he asked.

"No sir," Frank and Albert both replied.

"Well, if you wanted to, I'd let you each bag one on my ranch. Better give it some thought. Hardly anyone gets an invite to hunt Old Man Gardner's ranch. That's what everyone calls me, Old Man Gardner, right?"

"Well almost everyone", Frank said.

"Anyway, if you ain't hunters, you're curious enough to be out exploring these hills a lot." As Mr. Gardner pulled away in the pickup, he yelled back at Albert and Frank, "I've seen your tracks for months now down by the waterhole.

I knew it was you and Albert. I recognize them boots you wear as the same ones that made them tracks. Tryin' to get a look at that big coyote you was trailin', right?" And in a cloud of dust, Mr. Gardner headed for town.

"Old Mister Gardner doesn't miss much does he?" said Albert.

"Not much," said Frank, "but he doesn't like people on his ranch uninvited, either, on account of them shootin' up his stock tanks and windmills. But you heard him invite us on."

"Yeah, that's pretty special," Albert agreed.

Several days passed and the mornings were cold. Winter was coming. Papa pulled in through the gate and said he had just seen Mr. Gardner down the road with a busted radiator hose. He said he tried to help him but the old man wouldn't take any help.

In about an hour Mr. Gardner showed up out in front of Frank's adobe. "Is that offer still good on the coffee?" he asked. "I'm about half frozen."

"Welcome! Come in," exclaimed Mama. "There's plenty, and strong, too."

"Only way I like it," said Mr. Gardner.

"Frank, put that sack of hot, dried chiles and the beef jerky in Mr. Gardner's truck," Mama said.

Mr. Gardner drank two full cups of coffee and seemed embarrassed that he was so worn out and cold. "I got to get goin'," he said. "Say, by the way, Pancho, have you and Albert changed your minds about huntin' on my ranch? The deer season's about half over now and the deer are thick on my place.

"Albert and I are not hunters, Mr. Gardner," Frank replied.

"Most boys would give their eye teeth to hunt my ranch. Even my sons' friends ain't allowed, 'cause they got no respect for property and livestock. Well, most of 'em. But come on up anyway. Lots to see on my place for a boy like you. My boys never cared about huntin'. Didn't care about wildlife. Didn't care about cows. And I used to think they cared about me and the ranch, but they don't care about the ranch. I don't think they care much about me, either. Then I thought they cared only about my money, but I honestly don't believe they care about that, either. They just want to go their own way. One thing I will say. They all really cared about their mother when she was alive. She was very loving and very proud of all her boys. Well, come up, Pancho. Lots to do and see for guys like you and me."

A light snow was beginning to fall as Mr. Gardner slowly moved toward his truck. "Let's hope we get a good one," he called back. "Maybe they'll close school. Besides, we need the moisture." As he started his truck he yelled, "If it snows real good, I'll come get you in my pickup."

It must have snowed all night long, and it was still snowing early in the morning. Frank was up early, even earlier than his sisters, who were excited because they were sure the school buses wouldn't be running.

"No school today!" Frank's father said as he came into the house from his truck. "I heard it on the radio in the truck as I was warming the engine." Papa soon left, and Mama was busy in the kitchen preparing breakfast with Frank's sisters.

Beep, Beep, Beep!

"It's Mr. Gardner," Mama said, "Invite him in."

"You ready to go, Pancho?" Mr. Gardner yelled.

"It's still snowing," Frank said.

"All the better," answered Mr. Gardner. "Let's get going. We can eat later at my place."

I hope he can drive in the snow, Frank's mother thought. *Is he in such a hurry he can't wait for it to stop snowing?*

"What's the hurry, Mr. Gardner?" Frank asked as he got into the front seat of the truck.

"No real hurry. Just don't want to be to late for the show," he said. "See, them clouds are beginning to break and it's already nearly stopped snowing. How much snow you think we got last night, Pancho?" he questioned.

"I'd say at least six or seven inches."

"More like three, maybe four inches in the Organ Mountains, at most," he replied. "Snowfall is deceiving to most people. They usually notice the drifts and over-estimate the real amount. This snow is an early one and it's gonna melt real fast. In two days time, you won't see any snow except on the high peaks and canyons where the sun don't hit directly.

"We're almost there! The best view on the whole ranch. See, the skies are opening and the clouds are lifting over the mountains."

"Wow! That is a beautiful view," exclaimed Frank.

"Ain't it though!", agreed Mr. Gardner. "I ain't seen it like that in a few years. Sorry about

coming by your place so early this morning, but I had to see this just one more time. Timing is everything, Pancho. Got to be in the right place at the right time or miss it altogether. I thought you'd probably like to see it like I did when I was young."

"I have never seen it prettier than this," agreed Frank.

"I have," said Mr. Gardner.

"When?" Frank asked.

"When I was your age," Mr. Gardner answered.

"How could it be any prettier than this?" Frank asked.

"That's a darn good question, Pancho. It don't seem to get as hot in the summer, or as cold in the winter. Wind don't blow as hard as it used to. Don't rain as hard as it used to. Food don't taste as good as it used to. Don't sleep as sound as I used to. It's all in perspective. Everything is more intense when you're young!

"Say, are you and Albert still trying to get a look at that big coyote you was trackin?"

"Albert doesn't have the patience I do, Mr. Gardner. He thinks it's a waste of time," Frank replied.

"He's right in a way," Mr. Gardner said. "Does Albert think them tracks belong to a coyote?"

"I believe he really thinks they belong to a dog," Frank replied.

"Well, Albert's right again, in a way."

"What do you mean?" Frank asked.

"As far as gettin' a close look at that coyote, you and Albert together ain't ever going to see it! That coyote knows how often you've been down by the waterhole, which way you came in and which direction you left. It knows the scent of each of you and knows if there's one or two of you there. There's no critter smarter than an old coyote, at least not on this continent."

"Smarter than a wolf?" asked Frank.

"In my opinion it ain't even a close race. Coyotes are smarter. That don't mean smarter is better, it just means more adaptable, more survival skills. Once there was a natural place for wolves, but things got outta whack—buffalo was their food. When the buffalo were gone, you got hungry wolves. You put in cows where there's hungry wolves, they eat cows. It ain't their fault, they are wolves. They ain't like coyotes. Coyotes like mostly small rodents—mice, rabbits. Don't bother cows, least not normally. Now, sheep, that's a different story. But I ain't got no sheep or such, so the coyotes and me, we get along."

"What did you mean, Albert was partly right about dog tracks?" Frank asked.

"Well, the Navajo Indians had a name for the coyote. In English it translates to God's Dog. I think the Apache may have had the same name. These Indian names ain't always just fanciful names, either. Too much collective knowledge in Indian lore to be just brushed aside.. When I was younger I had different ideas; I thought differently. Now I can look back and see where I was dead wrong about a lot of things, and probably wrong about many others. Even now I am not so sure of anything anymore, except one thing!"

"What's that?" asked Frank

"God!" said Mr. Gardner. "That's all that I'm really sure of any more—God. Everything in my life has changed; I have changed, but God is, was, and will always be. God is the instrument of all change, but God never changes. Apaches called him *Ussen*. We call him *God*.

"There's a lot of Indian stories about the coyote. He is a very special animal to the Indians. A coyote has power. But, hearing them stories or readin' 'em ain't the same as seeing that POWER—knowing that POWER. Indians didn't write their history, they told stories to pass the knowledge from one generation to the next. Some of those stories probably have their roots thousands of years in the past.

"'The coyote will help you' is a statement still made by many Indians today. Why? Because it is accepted as truth through countless centuries of Indian lore. It is the power that is carried by the coyote that warrants his name of God's Dog. I have seen this power. It is very rare, very special, and very real. Pancho, I think you might be one of the very few to be lucky enough to see and feel this power, and I think I can help you. But if you do experience the coyote's power, it will have nothing to do with me or you. You will see and feel the power through God's Dog, but don't forget the power is that of God and not of this world. You will know if you are chosen to receive the power. When it is revealed, you will instantly know.

"Let's head for the ranch. We'll have us a good breakfast and see if we can get you started on your quest."

One coyote story took place east of El Paso at a place called Hueco Tanks, a series of natural basins located in the desert of West Texas. It is a story of the coyote as the carrier of good medicine.

A band of Kiowa warriors were overtaken by Mexican soldiers at Hueco Tanks and a bloody battle took place. One Kiowa was so badly wounded that he had to be hidden by his comrades and left near a spring. As the day passed and night advanced, he was near death.

In his state of half-consciousness, the warrior heard the distant howling of coyotes. The howling came nearer and the Indian was sure that the coyotes had smelled his blood and were only waiting for him to die before they began feasting. The next thing the Indian remembered was hearing soft footsteps close to his ear. A coyote came forward and licked his wounds, then laid down quietly by his side. This soothed the Indian and he fell asleep. When he awoke, the coyote was still lying by his side and would periodically lick his wounds. Soon, strength returned to the Kiowa brave and he managed to crawl to a spring to quench his thirst. The coyote "told" him that he must endure and that he would return to his people. That day Comanches (friends of the Kiowa) came to the spring and found the wounded warrior and returned him to the camp of his people.

At the next sun dance, the warrior made public his thanksgiving to the coyote. This story took place in 1839.*

In a short time they arrived at the ranch, Mr. Gardner opened the old door to the ranch house and they headed for the kitchen. He said, "It's just us two today. Rod's in Albuquerque with his Ag teacher. Seems there's a big livestock show and veterinary exhibit going on." As they passed through the main room in the ranch house, Frank's eyes fixed on the huge, old fireplace and the old, black smudges around its edges. "Go ahead and stir them coals. Should still be red hot, and throw a couple of the split logs on. Yeah, we'll have a nice, warm fire to eat our breakfast by." After what seemed like the biggest

*As told by James Mooney in *The Calendar History of the Kiowa Indians*, 17th Annual Report of the Bureau of American Ethnology, Part 1, Washington, D.C., 1898, pp. 302-305, as cited in *The Voice of the Coyote*, by J. Frank Dobie, Curtis Publishing Company, 1947.

breakfast Frank had ever eaten—eggs, tortillas, good ham, hot chile salsa, big biscuits with butter and grape jelly, and coffee—Mr. Gardner paused and stared at the now roaring fire.

"Yeah, coyotes are something when it comes to intelligence and cunning. They have native intelligence. It's born in 'em. They also have a great ability to learn. I could tell you coyote stories for a week, all kinds of stories about coyotes and coyote behavior. Many I heard as a boy, from my Dad or the other ranchers in the area. Some were old Indian stories, some personal experiences. I never really believed most of 'em, although I wanted to. I just figured they had to be made up. They just couldn't be true. That was a long time ago. I know better now. I still wouldn't believe them stories if I hadn't stayed in the ranching life.

"It's gonna' take some doin', but if you follow what I tell you and you do your part, God's Dog will either appear or he won't. Don't forget. The coyote is just the messenger.

"Now—that big coyote—he's the clan leader. He has all the territory from that waterhole to the other side of this ranch. The only other coyotes in that territory are his kin, either his mate, his pups, brothers and sisters, or those he chooses to accept. He won't tolerate other coyotes in his territory.

"Those other tracks you saw with Albert—those were of one of his half-grown pups. Male coyotes take a very active role in raising their young, and it's a lifelong bond, too. Now, I've given it a good bit of thought, and there's only one way to see that coyote closeup. How would you go about it, Pancho?"

"Hide so he couldn't tell I was there, I guess, and be perfectly still and quiet," Frank answered.

"Didn't you and Albert try that?" replied Mr. Gardner.

"Yeah, but he just never showed up."

"He's like a lot of things," Mr. Gardner said. "Just cause you can't see him don't mean he ain't there. You can bet he was there! He knew that both of you were there, hidin', motionless, perfectly quiet, trying to trick him into thinking you weren't there. He knew. The coyote's known as 'the Trickster,' and you were trying to out-trick him. It's quite a job to out-trick the Master Trickster."

"How can it be done, then?" asked Frank.

"Will you listen to this old man?" Mr. Gardner said as he lowered his eyes to meet Frank's.

"Yes, sir, I will," Frank answered excitedly.

"Well, good! A lot of folks won't, you know. You go down to that waterhole, be there about an hour before sundown. Don't get right to the water, stay off a little ways, show him you ain't interested in poisoning his water. Find you a comfortable spot to sit, and sit in a spot that's open. Be natural. Make no attempt to hide. Hum a tune if you like, or recite a poem. Don't matter. Wait there 'til the sun sets, then give it another fifteen minutes or so. Then if he ain't showed, just get up and go home. You'll still find the road home before dark. Repeat the same thing as soon as you can. Don't do nothin' different. Try not to miss more than one day, or two at the most. You've got to show him you're serious about meeting him. He'll know, and he'll know you mean him no harm."

"Try it for a week. See what happens. Don't forget! You'll either be chosen to receive the power, or there's nothing you can do to make it happen."

For the next three days, Frank did exactly as Mr. Gardner had said, and each time failed to see the old coyote. Somehow, though he didn't see anything, he felt he wasn't alone. As he walked down the rocky ranch road he could hear the howling of the coyotes communicating with each other in the distant hills.

As Frank walked in the door to his old adobe house, he heard his Father say, "Here he is. He's finally home!"

His Mother added, "Frank, where have you been? We've been looking for you. What in the world are you into these last few weeks? You are always off running around somewhere! Your Papa needs more of your help around here. He's been having to chop firewood and you know that's your job."

"Sorry, Mama, but I promise to finish chopping the wood tomorrow."

"We're ready to eat supper now," Papa said. "You eat, get to your room, and go to bed early. I want you to start on that wood early in the morning, and I want you to finish the job as soon as you get home from school tomorrow."

Frank finished his supper and then went to his room like his Father had said.

He felt guilty for getting behind in his chores, but knew it was best not to try to explain his actions to his parents. It would seem so foolish. His parents were well aware of Frank's interest in natural things. He had always been different that way, but since he had met Mr. Gardner, they were a little concerned about the old rancher's influence on the boy.

"What do you know about Mr. Gardner, about his life?" Mama asked of Papa.

"I've been asking about him to the neighboring families, those who have been here the longest. We've known him for years, yet we don't know him at all, really. It's the same with the others. They say he hardly ever engages in conversation, just hello, short replies, and off he goes. Some think he's mean, but that's just the younger generation. The ones that have known him the longest say he's just the opposite. He's a very kind man with a very rough manner. People don't understand him well."

"Well, for a man who doesn't say much, he sure talks to Frank," Mama observed.

Papa agreed, "Yes, he does. I think he understands him well. Ever notice how he never calls him Frank, always Pancho. That's a familiar name, a nickname, just like they were always close friends," Papa answered.

Papa continued, "I never said too much about him spending so much time out lately, 'cause I knew Mr. Gardner to be a good man and Frank likes him. The friendship is special for both of them."

"He's not teaching him to keep up with his chores, that's for sure," said Mama.

Papa assured her, "That's all settled now. He'll finish chopping that wood in the next couple of days. He's a good boy."

"Yeah, different though," said Mama. She looked at Papa sadly and said, "Do you think you should tell him that young Rod came by and said he had to take Mr. Gardner to the hospital, and how sick he is?"

Papa shook his head and replied, "No, everyone knows something's been wrong with his health the last year or so. Rumors going around in Las Cruces say it's his heart. I've been patient with Frank lately 'cause I felt Mr. Gardner wanted to teach him something and he's been such a lonely man for so long. I'll tell him in the morning. He needs to sleep soundly tonight. I noticed Rod made a special effort to find Frank and tell him about his sick Papa. He knows how close his Papa and Frank have become lately. I think Rod is a little hurt, or jealous, maybe."

"Maybe so," said Mama.

For the next two days Frank was too busy with school and chopping firewood for anything else. During the day, and especially at night, he thought about Mr. Gardner.

"I said a special prayer for Mr. Gardner," his Mama told him, "it wouldn't hurt if you did the same; he's very sick."

"I have, Mama, but I just know everything's going to be all right, no matter what happens," Frank told her.

"I know you've got a lot on your mind, son. You've been a little quiet the last few days. You sure did a good job on choppin' and stackin' all that firewood. I guess there's other things you'd like to do now," his Father said.

"Yes sir, but I won't be home 'til after dark," he told his Father.

"Just make sure it's not too long after dark. Your Mama worries so."

"I promise," Frank said.

Frank had been sitting in the open for more that an hour, just like before, concentrating his thoughts on God's Dog and thinking of Mr. Gardner. Sometimes he would hum a little tune or just talk quietly to himself. Once or twice he saw something move out of the bushes, but it was only another jackrabbit.

The sky was changing colors fast now, the shadows were very long and the sun would soon be going down. Now the light was slipping away, and the last edge of the sun would soon be dropping below the western sky. Frank was tempted to get up and start the long walk home, but then he remembered what Old Man Gardner had said: "Will you listen to an Old Man? Wait fifteen minutes or so after sundown before you give up and leave." Frank stared at the open space between the creosote bushes, not more than six feet in front of him. It was the last, dim light of day. Soon it would be dark.

Then there He was, in the open, staring directly into Frank's eyes...

Strangely, Frank stared back directly into the eyes of the biggest ol' coyote he had ever seen. He thought he would act differently if something like this ever happened, but he was very calm and felt a reassurance and peace he had never felt before. The coyote stood very still and seemed to stare into Frank's very soul. They remained staring at each other for what seemed like a long time, but was probably only five seconds, no more than ten at the very most. Then He disappeared into the dark shadows and the creosote bushes.

Frank's excitement was very strong, but a sense of incredible joy took its place immediately. *I have seen the Power! I have been chosen!*

When he reached home he could hardly think of anything but the end of the most perfect day he had ever known. He wanted to tell his parents so badly, but felt they probably wouldn't share his great joy at his telling of his encounter. His mother was opening the door as he stepped onto the old, wooden porch.

"You may as well come and sit down. Your Papa has some bad news to tell you."

With deep concern, Papa looked at Frank and said, "Mr. Gardner has gotten worse. His boys are all coming home. Rod said one of his older brothers is here already, the other two are on their way. Doc Miller says he can't live but a few days, at best, but he is in no pain. He seems excited. Doc Miller said he's a very tough old man, but he's just worn out. He sent a message to you. Says he wants you to kind of help Rod for a few days, if you can. Make sure all the ranch gates aren't left wide open. He thinks Rod gets too careless when he ain't watched over. Doc says he wants you to bring him some carne seca and visit him as soon as possible. Doc says he will only allow you to bring him a piece or two of that jerky—says it won't hurt him, but he doesn't want him using his last strength chewing dried beef. He says the old man wants to spend a few minutes alone with you, but Doc doesn't want him having any visitors for a day or two. He's that sick."

The next day was a regular school day, but Frank couldn't concentrate on anything that day. After school he headed straight home, and when he got there his sisters were running and laughing just like they always did. His mother was in the kitchen.

"Mama, any news about Mr. Gardner?" Frank asked.
"No, there's been no news today," she replied, then added, "Find something to do. Your sisters and I are going to clean the house."
"I may walk up the road about a mile or so," Frank said.
"Now don't be going back to that waterhole at this time of day, it's just too far," his Mother warned him.

"I'm not, Mama, I just thought I'd walk up to the ridge; it's not that far."

"Your Papa will be late this evening, but you better be home before he gets here."

"I will," Frank promised.

It was getting late in the day now. The sun was already low in the sky. Just over the ridge was the eastern boundary of the Gardner ranch, with the mountains in the near distance. Frank thought that he would just sit and rest for a few minutes, then head back before his Papa got home. Looking at the mountains on Mr. Gardner's ranch, beyond the ridge, he watched the colors change from gold to red and soft pink.

Then, there He was, not twenty feet from Frank, framed against the distant pink mountains—God's Dog! This time the ol' coyote seemed almost to smile at Frank as he stood there for the longest time, as proud and beautiful as anything Frank had ever seen. Then He was gone and the pink faded away, and it grew dark almost before his eyes. Frank headed for home with great excitement.

Just as Frank was almost in front of his house, he saw his Father's old pickup, with the headlights on, stop at the mailbox down the road. He waited by the house for his Papa to drive up. As his Father got out of the truck, he was holding up a note.

"Looks like news about Mr. Gardner. Let's go inside and let your Mama read it," Papa said.

Mama looked at the note silently, then solemnly said, "Rod wants you to go in with him in the morning to the hospital."

"Can I, Mama?" Frank asked.

"Tomorrow is a school day," she replied, "but I guess this is more important."

"He can make up his school work," said Papa.

"Well, all right, but be ready early, Rod says, and remember to take some carne seca," his Mother reminded him.

Frank was up early the next day and even drank a cup of coffee with his Papa.

"When did you start drinking coffee?" Papa asked. "Well, I guess you're old enough."

Beep! Beep!

"Let's go," yelled Rod, "I'm sure Dad's waitin'".

"Don't forget the carne seca," Mama said.

On the way into town Rod told Frank that he and his three brothers had spent all the day before and most of the night with their Dad. "We had a lot of things to say to him," said Rod, "and surprisingly he had a lot to say to us, but he especially asked that I bring you in this morning."

As soon as Frank walked into the hospital room, slowly closing the door, he heard from behind the curtain, "That ought to be Pancho now!" from the bed on the other side.

"Don't let him get too excited, son," whispered Doc Miller.

The voice from behind the curtain sounded again, "You boys go get ya' a Coke or something. You go with 'em, Doc. Put it on my tab," the old man said jokingly. As soon as the door closed, Frank handed him a piece of jerky.

"Put that on the table. I'll eat it later. Tell me, boy! Tell me!"

Frank was wide-eyed and trying to make the words come. Mr. Gardner interrupted, "I know you saw and felt the Power! I knew, if anyone would, you would."

Frank finally found the words, "You wouldn't believe it, Mr. Gardner. Right in front of me, nearly as close as we are now."

Mr. Gardner was quick to answer, "All right, all right, you don't have to convince me. But what I want to know is about yesterday evening, about sundown. You saw him again, didn't you?"

"Well, yes, but how could you possibly know that?" asked Frank.

"I saw him through your eyes, boy, that's how! I was lyin' here in bed just looking at the ceiling, and suddenly there He was, not twenty feet away. Right? The eastern boundary of my ranch, that's where he was. Had a coyote grin on like he was smilin'! Stood there a long time, too, proud as he could be."

"Exactly, Mr Gardner! But how could you know?" Frank asked in bewilderment.

Mr. Gardner answered, "I told you, I seen 'im through your eyes! See, he's God's Dog, but he's only the messenger. He passed you the message to bring to me. That's my message, sent to me. Even though I saw it too, you was seein' it for real. You was supposed to pass it on to me, otherwise I might have thought I had a premonition, or some such thing. No, I got my message, as direct as any Western Union ever sent."

It seemed like Frank had been there such a short time when Doc Miller came in and motioned for Frank to go.

"See ya, Mr. Gardner," Frank said.

"You betcha!" Mr. Gardner replied weakly.

As soon as Frank got off the school bus the next day, he saw Albert and some of the other boys. Albert came running over and asked, "Did you ever see that coyote?"

"I sure did," Frank replied.

"I knew you would if anyone would. Was he as big as I said?" questioned Albert.

"Bigger," Frank answered.

"Gosh, I wish I could've seen him with you." Albert said.

"Mr. Gardner said that it wouldn't happen if the two of us were there." replied Frank.

"I guess you heard," Albert said.

"Heard what?" Frank asked.

"Old Man Gardner died last night," Albert said. The bell rang and school started for another day.

Two days passed and Albert and Frank were saddling up the old horses at Frank's place, when down the road came Rod driving his father's beat-up truck. He stopped and slowly climbed out of the truck, took off his hat and said, "Well, Frank, we buried Pa on the ranch yesterday, just like he wanted. It all happened so fast. He didn't want no special funeral or nothin', just bury him and get it over with. You know how he was about puttin' things off. Anyway, Pa died during the night, peacefully in his sleep. I want to thank you for helping him during his last few days."

Frank spoke quietly, "I really didn't do much."

"Well, Dad felt he could count on you to help. Only had a few at the services. That's the way he wanted it. Just me, my brothers, a couple of the old timers and Father Thomas," Rod explained.

Albert spoke out, "I didn't know you were Catholic."

"We aren't," Rod replied. "Dad always told us he didn't care what denomination we were, just as long as we were Christians. Father Thomas said he had always known Dad to be that. No matter what happened in his life, good or bad, he was always a Christian. Seems the last ten years or so Dad was helping Father Thomas feed and clothe some of them boys at the Catholic Boys School. It was all news to us."

"Anyway," Rod continued, "the real reason I'm down here is to deliver that old trunk in the back of the pickup. Dad wanted you to have it. Don't know what you would want with it, though. Ain't nothing in it but a few pieces of old ranch junk. An old, broken down six shooter, an old rusty spur without its mate, a bunch of old written-down stories,

all wrapped together and yellowed with age. Just junk!"

"Thanks, Rod," Frank managed to say.

"I don't know if you'd be interested in helpin' me around the ranch a little now and again, if I need it," Rod asked of Frank. "Course it would mean a little extra money for you."

"Well, Rod, if you ever get in a real bind, I'll help you if I can, but I don't think you're gonna need me," was Frank's answer.

"Thanks, Frank. You and Albert are always welcome on the Gardner Ranch! Lots to see and do on the ranch for boys like you. Did you ever see the Indian writing on the rocks?"

"No, I never did," said Frank.

"About a mile up that canyon from the waterhole."

"What kind of writing?" Albert asked.

"Petroglyphs. Been there for centuries. Maybe even longer. Just a bunch of footprints and animal tracks carved in the rocks."

"Can you tell what it means?" asked Albert.

"Nah, probably don't mean nothin', least not to me. My Dad once told me an old Indian story about 'em, but I don't remember it now. I never paid no attention to them stories he used to tell."

Frank asked, "What kind of animal tracks are they?"

"Oh, if I remember, there's human hands and feet, deer tracks and coyote, I think. The story had something to do with Indian beliefs, power, coyotes and such. I just don't remember. Just an old Indian story. Don't mean nothin'. Well, I've got to get goin'." Rod backed up the pickup and started down the road when he came to a sudden stop. "Whoops, almost forgot! I got something else for you."

He reached in the glove compartment of his pickup and pulled out a crumpled piece of paper. "Doc Miller found it in Dad's hand when he died. Hope you don't mind, but I read it. It's the last few words of the Lord's Prayer, I think," Rod said. "Don't know quite what he meant to say to you. Well, I'll be seeing you," he called, then hurried down the rocky road toward the ranch.

To Pancho,
For Thine is the
kingdom and the
POWER and the
Glory Forever.

Some Interesting Words and Phrases

Adaptable: Able to adjust to different conditions

Adobe: Sun-dried bricks made of mud, clay and straw, used for building houses in the Southwestern United States and Mexico; also the resulting architectural style

Ag teacher: A slang term used for a teacher of agriculture or farming and ranching

Albuquerque: The largest city in New Mexico; located in central New Mexico, the Rio Grande river runs through it

Apache Indians: A Native American tribe adapted to the harsh desert conditions of the American Southwest

Arroyo: A Spanish word meaning a watercourse in a dry region

Badger: A carniverous burrowing mammal with short legs, long claws on the front feet, and a heavy, grizzled coat

Bag one: A slang phrase meaning to kill an animal

Beef jerky: Naturally dried, seasoned beef eaten by early settlers and travelers, yesterday and today

Bind: To tie or wrap tightly

Boot heel: When seen on a map of the state, Southwestern New Mexico resembles the heel of a boot

Boundary: The limit of a territory or area; a border

Buffalo: A large, shaggy-maned North American bovine; once roamed the plains in huge herds

Burrito: A Mexican food consisting of a soft flour tortilla rolled around a filling such as beef, beans, potatoes, etc., and eaten like a sandwich

Cactus: Any of a variety of drought-resistant flowering plants with succulent stems and sharp spikes or spines

Canyon: A deep, narrow valley with high, steep sides

Carne seca: Spanish for dried beef or beef jerky

Chile: One of a variety of strong, often spicy peppers related to the tomato; may be combined with meats, beans, onion, garlic, etc. to make a dish of the same name

Clan leader: The chief or primary individual in a group of animals having ties to a common ancestor

Coals: Burned embers of wood, charcoal

Continent: Any of the large land mass divisions of the earth; e.g. the North American continent

Coyote: A small canine of North America, related to but smaller than the wolf

Creosote: A resinous shrub of the western United States and Mexico that exudes a very distinctive odor which is especially pungent during a rainstorm

Critter: Slang term for any of a variety of small animals

Cunning: Marked by wiliness and trickery

Deer are thick: A western term used to imply a large quantity of deer in a specific area

Denomination: A religious term that designates a unity of several congregations of similar beliefs

Herd: A group of animals that live together

Horned toad: Any of several small, harmless lizards with spines on the head that resemble horns

Indian lore: Stories and tales passed from generation to generation in various North American Indian tribes

Jackrabbit: A desert mammal with extremely long ears that radiate body heat and allow the animal to survive the hot, dry deserts of the American Southwest; a member of the Hare family

Kin: Relatives

Lizard: A four-legged reptile with a long, tapering tail

Lobo: The Spanish word for wolf; also the Mexican gray wolf once common in the Southwest; feeds primarily on large, hoofed mammals such as buffalo, deer, and elk

Messenger: One who carries a message; a prophet

Mesilla Valley: A large, fertile agricultural area of the Rio Grande river in Southern New Mexico

Moisture: A small amount of liquid that causes dampness; also a term in the western states referring to rainfall

Mountain lion: Cougar; a large, powerful tawny-brown wild American cat that preys on other animals

Much obliged: A western term expressing appreciation

Natural: Of, relating to, or concerning nature; faithfully representing life or nature

Navajo Indians: A Native American people, believed to be descended from the early Anasazi, who live in Western New Mexico and Arizona

Organ Mountains: A small mountain range formed by a volcanic up-thrust, defining the eastern boundary of the Mesilla Valley; named for the peaks, which resemble organ pipes; the tallest is over 9,000 ft.

Perspective: A view of things in their true relationship or relative importance; a point of view

Petroglyphs: Ancient rock carvings and symbols found in many places in the American Southwest

Pickup: A light truck having an enclosed cab and an open bed with low sides and a tailgate

Quail: Short-winged small game birds related to the domestic chicken

Quest: Mission or spiritual journey

Radiator hose: Rubber tubing that allows water to circulate between the engine and radiator in an automobile

Ranch: A large farm, especially in the American West, devoted to raising livestock such as cattle, sheep or horses

Rattlesnake: Any of several venomous American pit vipers with segments called "rattles" at the end of the tail

Recite: To present orally

Reliable: Trustworthy, dependable

Ridge: A crest, or a long, narrow land elevation at the top of a hill or a mountain

Rio Grande: Long river originating in the Rocky Mountains of Colorado, flowing south through New Mexico; forms the boundary between Texas and Mexico before emptying into the Gulf of Mexico

Roadrunner: New Mexico's state bird, this fast runner is found in the Southwestern United States and Mexico

Rodent: Small mammal (mouse, squirrel, beaver) with sharp front teeth for gnawing

Robledo Mountains: A small range of mountain peaks on the western side of the Rio Grande that form the northwestern boundary of the Mesilla Valley

Sack: A large bag made of heavy cloth, used for holding items in bulk

Salsa: A spicy sauce of tomatoes, onions, and chiles

Scent: Odor or smell

Six shooter: A pistol with a revolving chamber that holds six bullets

Smudge: A dirty or blurred spot

Spell: A period of physical distress

Split logs: Firewood made by splitting a log in pieces lengthwise for easier, more efficient burning

Stock tanks: Galvanized steel tanks used for watering livestock in arid country, filled with water pumped by windmills or electric pumps; also man-made ponds filled with rain runoff and/or well water

Stockman: A rancher

Survival skills: Learned or innate abilities used to escape or avoid harm in natural settings; necessary for "living off the land"

Territory: An area occupied and defended by one or a group of animals

Tortilla: A thin, round bread of unleavened cornmeal or wheat flour served with most Mexican meals

Veterinary exhibit: A display of medicines, medical instruments, and procedures used to treat animals

Washboard: A corrugated sheet of metal fixed inside of a wooden frame and used to rub clothes while washing; a dirt road with a similar rough surface

Waterhole: A depression in the ground or rock, filled with water to which animals come to drink

Windmill: A machine mounted on a high tower with a "wheel" made of sails which catch the wind, turning and making the motor pump water from a deep well

Hasta La Vista!: A Spanish phrase meaning "'Til We See You Again!"

A Note to Parents & Teachers

Pancho and the Power is a story that very accurately portrays the life and adventures of a young boy growing up in a rural setting in the desert Southwest, near the U.S./Mexico border. Pancho's quest for the coyote is a spiritual one, similar to those done by Native American youth as they approach adulthood. The story incorporates references to a variety of animals, plants, and geography, all beautifully illustrated with the author's photographs.

Encourage children to ask questions as they read the story. Refer to the included glossary and look for more complete explanations by referring to encyclopedias and other books.

There are many topics that might intrigue young people and photographs that will catch their eyes. These can be used as subjects for reports and additional reading assignments or explorations of the unique features of the American Southwest.